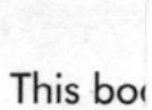
This bo

I celebrated World Book Day 2018

with this brilliant gift from my local bookseller,

&

GERARD SIGGINS

CELEBRATE STORIES. LOVE READING.

This book has been specially written and published to celebrate **World Book Day**. We are a charity who offers every child and young person the opportunity to read and love books by offering you the chance to have a book of your own. To find out more – as well as oodles of fun activities and reading recommendations to continue your reading journey, visit **worldbookday.com**

World Book Day in the UK and Ireland is made possible by generous sponsorship from National Book Tokens, participating publishers, booksellers, authors and illustrators. The €1.50 book tokens (£1 in the UK) are a gift from your local bookseller.

World Book Day works in partnership with a number of charities, all of whom are working to encourage a love of reading for pleasure.

Suas are an Irish children's literacy charity. They have a simple but powerful belief – literacy changes everything. Founded in Ireland in 2002, Suas works with disadvantaged children in Ireland, India, Zambia and Kenya.

In Ireland, their trained volunteers provide one-to-one reading and maths mentoring to children in disadvantaged schools. To date, Suas have helped over 3,300 children from the most disadvantaged communities in Ireland to improve their literacy skills. **www.suas.ie**

Children's Books Ireland/Leabhair Pháistí Eireann is Ireland's national children's books organisation. Through their many activities and events they aim to engage young people with books, foster a greater understanding of the importance of books for young people and act as a hub for families, schools, libraries and communities with an interest in books for children in Ireland.

CBI's goal is to make books central to every child's life on the island of Ireland through raising awareness, developing audiences and celebrating excellent authors and illustrators. **childrensbooksireland.ie**

GERARD SIGGINS was born in Dublin and has lived almost all his life in the shadow of Lansdowne Road; he's been attending rugby matches there since he was small enough for his dad to lift him over the turnstiles. He is a sports journalist and worked for the *Sunday Tribune* for many years.

Other books about rugby player Eoin Madden by Gerard Siggins

Rugby Spirit
Rugby Warrior
Rugby Rebel
Rugby Flyer
Rugby Runner
Rugby Heroes

RUGBY ROAR

GERARD SIGGINS

THE O'BRIEN PRESS
DUBLIN

First published 2018 by
The O'Brien Press Ltd.,
12 Terenure Road East, Rathgar,
Dublin 6, Ireland
D06 HD27
Tel: +353 1 4923333; Fax: +353 1 4922777
E-mail: books@obrien.ie.
Website: www.obrien.ie
The O'Brien Press is a member of Publishing Ireland.

ISBN: 978-1-78849-002-3

1 3 5 7 6 4 2
18 20 22 21 19

Printed and bound by CPI Group (UK) Ltd, Croydon, CR0 4YY
The paper in this book is produced using pulp from managed forests.

Published in
DUBLIN
UNESCO
City of Literature

DEDICATION

Since I started writing the Eoin Madden rugby book series I have had wonderful support and encouragement from many people – everyone at The O'Brien Press, librarians, booksellers, teachers, parents, and, most importantly, readers. I'd like to dedicate *Rugby Roar* to them all with my never-ending thanks.

ACKNOWLEDGEMENTS

Many thanks to Susan for 'coming off the bench' and stepping into the world of Eoin Madden so skillfully. And thanks to Aedeen and John, my friends in New Zealand, for helping me paint the pictures – I hope to see you there some day.

CHAPTER 1

Eoin Madden hated fuss, which wasn't good, as fuss seemed to enjoy following him around. Besides being a star rugby player for his school, province and country, he had also been at the centre of two major news stories in just over a year, and his grinning face was well-known to readers of every newspaper and viewer of TV news.

But worse than the public attention, and worse even than being pestered for selfies by every first-year pupil at Castlerock College, was when he had to get dressed up for a big occasion.

Eoin liked nothing better than lounging around in a tracksuit, or a hoodie. The whole buttoned-up shirt, tie and blazer thing made him feel uncomfortable. So, when he saw the words 'neat dress essential' on an invitation, he always tried to find a way out of accepting.

He was never mad keen on getting official-looking letters, but he couldn't dodge the post he received one morning on his way to class.

'Madden,' called the headmaster, Mr McCaffrey, as he crossed the entrance hall before the first period of the day. 'The postman has just been and he delivered this for you … it's from the IRFU.'

Eoin thanked his headmaster as he handed over the white envelope, but there was no way he was going to open the letter in front of the head and a crowd of classmates. He slipped it inside his French book and headed for the languages room on the second floor.

Eoin wondered what might be inside, but as the rugby season was over he reckoned it was probably nothing important and quickly forgot about it for several hours, until school was finished for the day.

As usual, he was lounging around the dormitory chatting with Alan, Dylan and Rory when the conversation came around to the summer holidays and what they had planned once their Junior Cert exams were over.

'I have a job lined up in the supermarket,' sighed Dylan. 'I have to give Mam a hand paying for stuff.'

Rory stretched out on the bed and vowed he would spend as much of the summer sleeping as he was allowed, while Alan didn't say anything and was looking uncomfortable as he stared at the floor.

'What's this, Alan? Why so quiet?' pushed Eoin. 'What are you up to?'

'Well …' replied his pal, 'I've signed up for a course.'

'Swot!' roared Dylan, tossing a pillow at Alan, who dodged out of the way and laughed as it hit Rory.

'It's not a study course,' Alan snapped. 'It's

… it's … a rugby thing. A mixture of learning how to be a match analyst and some basic coaching too. I'm going to go for my badges.'

'That's pretty cool, Al,' smiled Eoin. 'You were really good at spotting things for us this year. Where is it on?'

'It's in Dublin somewhere, probably one of the universities. It's run by the IRFU …'

That was the moment when Eoin remembered that IRFU letter, and his pals saw him smack himself on the side of the head and start rooting in his schoolbag.

'Got it,' he grinned, extracting the white envelope from the French textbook.

'Is that from the IRFU?' asked Alan, spying the logo printed on the envelope as Eoin slit it open with his pencil.

'It is,' he replied, starting to read. 'Blah, blah, blah, Four Nations, blah, blah, World Cup, blah, bl—'

Eoin stopped short, and his eyes bulged.

He looked up at Alan, and across to Dylan and Rory. He gulped again, and cleared his throat.

'You won't believe this, lads, but they've just gone and selected me for the British and Irish Lions. And we're going on tour to New Zealand!'

CHAPTER 2

With his friends' congratulations ringing in his ears, Eoin decided to read the letter again. World Rugby and the home unions had been delighted by the success of the Under 16 World Cup, and the tournament with Wales, England, Scotland and Ireland was also very popular with TV viewers. They had initially decided to select a team of the Four Nations Tournament just to honour the best players, but when, late one night, a New Zealand union official rang his Irish counterpart and offered to host a junior Lions side, the idea quickly gathered pace.

'The coaches of the four sides convened last weekend and selected a squad of thirty-three players that will play three games against various New Zealand state schoolboy sides, as well as two Test matches against the Baby Blacks.

'We have selected you as vice-captain and request that you make yourself available between the dates below. Please attend at the hotel below, this Friday, for the public announcement of the tour and the names of the rest of the squad. Neat dress essential.'

'Vice-captain,' Eoin gasped. 'And "neat dress essential".'

'That certainly beats working in Shopsco for the summer,' grumbled Dylan, although he did manage a grin when he looked up at Eoin.

'Ah Dyl, don't be like that. I promise I'll send you a postcard,' Eoin grinned back.

Rory looked uncomfortable, but said nothing. He had been part of the Ireland team but because he hadn't received a letter he presumed he wasn't going to New Zealand. Eoin nodded to him and shrugged his shoulders.

'Maybe the post will come tomorrow?' he suggested. 'You're in with a great shout. You're better than nearly all the other scrum-halves.'

Dylan and Alan agreed, but Rory just smiled thinly and left the room.

Eoin lay back on his bed and read the letter again. He was stunned to receive such amazing news, but a bit worried at the disruption and distraction it would cause to his studies. There were just five weeks to the exams, and the tour party flew out two days after they were over. Getting organised would be important, and he would be wrecked after the exams. Maybe he would get to sleep on the plane.

He jumped off the bed and grabbed a hoodie. 'I'm going to ring my folks,' he told his room-mates, 'and maybe take a jog too.'

Because it was proving a big distraction to many, Castlerock had banned mobile phones for the two months leading up to the exams. That meant Eoin had to use the old phone box that stood in the hall outside Mr McCaffrey's office. Even with the ban, almost nobody used it, so Eoin was surprised to see that the booth was occupied.

He hung around for a few minutes until the door opened, and out stepped Charlie Bermingham.

'Eoin!' he grinned. 'What are you here for – not the same as me, are you?'

'Well that depends,' said Eoin, cagily.

'Did you get a letter from the IRFU?' asked Charlie.

'Yes! Are you going to New Zealand too?'

'I am. Amazing, isn't it? I was just telling my dad there.'

'Yeah, that's what I'm here for too. I have to go to some function this week – they've made me vice-captain.'

'Really? That's great news – I'm the captain!'

The pair laughed again and congratulated each other before Eoin slipped into the phone box to ring his parents.

They were naturally overjoyed, but Eoin was even more delighted when his mother asked him would he like to talk to the visitor who had just arrived.

'Dixie!' he called, once he recognised the voice. His grandad, who they all called 'Dixie', had been a famous rugby player and was always a great help to Eoin as he made his way in the game.

Eoin filled Dixie in on what he knew about the tour and asked would his grandad be able to travel to watch the games.

'Are you joking, Eoin?' Dixie laughed. 'It's about 12,000 miles away! I wouldn't have the energy for that amount of travel. But I'll listen out for your scores on the radio.'

Eoin laughed back. 'I suppose it is a long way away, but you've been a lucky charm for me at all my games.'

'Well, you'll have to get used to me not being there,' chuckled Dixie. 'I won't be here forever, you know.'

'Don't say that, Grandad,' said Eoin. 'You've plenty of years left in you. Which is more than I can say about my Junior Cert study. Say good night to Mam and Dad, will you? I've got to get back to my books.'

CHAPTER 3

A few days later Eoin and Charlie were paraded in front of the media at the unveiling of what they had decided to call 'The British and Irish Lion Cubs Tour'. They were the only two players there, so they got a lot of attention, and Eoin had to fend off lots of questions about his adventures while playing for Ireland.

'Only Lion Cubs questions, please,' said the PR lady, and Eoin was happy to keep saying that whenever a journalist went off the subject.

He and Charlie had turned up in their Ireland blazers but were ushered into a side room where they were fitted with blue blazers with the famous crest of England, Ireland, Scotland and Wales. They grinned at each other, realising they were now part of one of the most exclusive clubs in rugby.

Some of the other players were interviewed by video link, so they got to learn who had been selected too: the English giant Edward Wood was there, and Scotland's Alistair Dods, as well as Owain Morgan from Wales.

The announcer said they would be bringing thirty-three players, to cover midweek games and allow everyone a chance to get some time on the field.

Charlie and Eoin were most interested in seeing which of their team-mates had been selected, though they reckoned that as Ireland were champions there would have to be at least ten in the squad.

The backs were named first, and Eoin was delighted that Matthew Peak, Dan Boyd, Kuba Nowak, Paddy O'Hare and his schoolmate Rory would be joining him in the squad.

'What do you reckon, Charlie?' he asked,

as they prepared to unveil the forwards. 'I reckon we'll get the whole back row: Seán Nolan and the Savage brothers.'

However, Charlie wasn't quite on the money with his selection. He, Noah Steenson and Oisín Deegan were picked as the 6-7-8 unit, but only Roger Savage had been selected in the second row.

'Poor George – he'll be devastated,' said Eoin. 'I've never seen him and Roger apart. Roger might even decide not to go.'

The surprise was that the whole Ireland front row had been selected too: props Seán Nolan and John Young, and hooker James Brady.

On their way back to school Eoin and Charlie were still buzzing about the selections. Eoin looked out the window as the Dart train neared Aviva Stadium. There was still building work going on, but he smiled as he remembered the great games he had played there for Castlerock and Ireland.

It was dark when they got back to school. Charlie stretched out his arms and said goodnight, but Eoin knew his bed wouldn't be welcoming him just yet. He had promised himself he would do two hours history revision tonight and the Lion Cubs function had got in the way.

He was delighted that his room-mates were asleep as that saved him the time he would have spent recounting the events of the evening. Rory had fallen asleep sitting up, trying to stay awake.

He spent most of the two hours reading under the lamplight about the First World War, which brought his mind back to Dave Gallaher, the Irish-born captain of the All Blacks whose ghost had appeared to Eoin. He smiled as he remembered how Dave had helped him with a school project that had won great praise. It would be good to visit the country where he had made his home.

Eoin's eyes grew heavy and he knew it was

time for sleep. Just before he hopped into bed he scribbled a note and left it on Rory's nightstand. It contained just two words, but he knew it would cheer him up in the morning.

'You're in.'

CHAPTER 4

The Junior Cert exams went better than Eoin expected, but he had so little time before he left for New Zealand that he didn't have a chance to visit Ormondstown, his home town in Tipperary. His parents came up to Dublin to say goodbye, and Dixie tagged along too.

'I was looking at the old globe at home and I reckon New Zealand is about as far as you can get from Ireland,' chuckled the old man.

'It is,' said Eoin. 'We did it in geography. If you push a giant needle through the centre of the earth from Dublin, it will come out in the sea about three hundred kilometres south of New Zealand. It's called its antipode.'

'Well now, that's interesting. I don't

imagine you will be taking a trip way out there in the ocean, but it will be nice to be close to it. There'll be plenty of other things to see there.'

'I know, but we don't have much time – we have five days to get over the jet lag before our first game, and then it's Saturday, Wednesday, Saturday, every week. We'll be home in three weeks.'

'Well, I hope you do well and enjoy the opportunity. I never got any further from home playing rugby than a friendly in Ballymena, so make sure you savour the culture and people you meet,' Dixie added.

Eoin hugged his family and waved again as he made his way into the Departures area in Dublin Airport. He had been told to travel light, so he just had a backpack, inside which he had his two favourite pairs of boots and a couple of books, and of course he had his phone tucked safely in the pocket of his new Lions blazer. Everything else he would wear and use over the next month would be provided by the Lions.

The Cubs who lived around Dublin were waiting for the plane to London: Charlie, Rory, Noah, Oisín, Kuba, Seán and James. The rest of the squad would fly from Belfast, Shannon or Cork.

Eoin joined the group, where the talk was all about 24-hour flights and what food would be served on the plane. Seán and James stocked up on chocolate bars, just in case.

Eoin sat with Charlie for the short flight, and the pair discussed what might be in store. England's Under-16 coach, Geoff, had been appointed coach for the tour, while Neil, who had coached Ireland all season, was one of his assistants.

'It seems a bit weird that Neil wasn't made coach, doesn't it?' Eoin asked Charlie. 'We won everything we entered!'

'Well … I suppose they couldn't have a coach and captain from the same country

– the team is supposed to represent all four nations, of course.

'Geoff seems like a nice guy and he's a good coach. He'll have other coaches to help him and he'll pick the best team. At least, I hope he will.'

CHAPTER 5

Players and coaches from all over Britain and Ireland gathered in the departure lounge at Heathrow. They had arrived togged out in blazers, but were given two huge red bags full of kit and told to change into a polo shirt and tracksuit for the long flight Down Under.

Eoin pulled the red shirt over his head and admired himself in a mirror. 'A Lion,' he said quietly, still surprised at how far he had come in just four years playing the sport.

Geoff called them all to order and made some announcements about the flight and the tour ahead. 'Right, I don't mind who you sit beside on the flight as long as he's from a different country. We're going out here as one party, so forget the "Wales" or "England" in brackets beside your name – and use the flight to get to know your team-mates.'

He introduced each of the coaches, and called up Charlie and Eoin too as captain and vice.

'But now I will announce the most important job on the tour. The Lions always give this to the youngest member of the party, and so we shall too.'

He delved into a kitbag and removed a huge cuddly lion cub.

'This is BIL,' he announced, 'which stands for British and Irish Lion. And he will come everywhere with us over the next few weeks. He must not be lost, under peril of severe fines. And you must all take responsibility for him, especially the Keeper of BIL, who will be ... Paddy O'Hare!'

Paddy looked as if he had been told he was going home. Everyone had heard the stories about the Lion Keeper and how his life was made a nightmare by pranksters who liked nothing more than kidnapping and hiding BIL. Paddy tucked him under his arm and rejoined his team-mates, who immediately tried to snatch him away.

It wasn't much better on the flight, and Paddy eventually had to ask the stewards to lock BIL up, to prevent him being taken.

Eoin sat beside Ed Wood on the plane, and they chatted about school life and rugby in Ireland and England.

'What do you make of Geoff?' asked Eoin.

'He's not bad,' replied Ed, 'but he can be a bit serious at times. He was really desperate for us to win the thing in Dublin so he was angry when you guys took it away. He takes it all a bit personally, I think.'

Eoin nodded. 'Sorry about that,' he grinned.

Ed laughed. 'I don't blame you for winning and, anyway, we're all on the same side now.'

CHAPTER 6

Even with a brief stop-over in Melbourne, Eoin couldn't believe how long the plane journey took, and was delighted when it came to an end after taking a full day out of his life. He had been warned about jetlag so had drunk several litres of water on the flight, and went for the three-hour nap that Geoff had ordered the boys to take as soon as they checked into their hotel in Auckland.

But, even having taken all the precautions, he felt tired and irritable when he got up and joined the team for a late lunch in the hotel. He sat with Rory and Tayo Okoro, one of the Scots lads, but as soon as he finished he excused himself.

'I've a bit of a headache,' he said. 'I'm going to go for a run.'

With that, he left the hotel, turned left and jogged for about five minutes before he realised he had lost his bearings and would need to get back to the team base. He looked up, hoping to catch something on the skyline that he would remember from the bus journey into the city, and was delighted to see the towering clear glass structure that was Eden Park, just a couple of blocks away.

He had been looking forward to seeing the ground that had hosted two World Cup finals, because the final Test of the Cubs series would be held there. He knew that to play there would be an unbelievable honour – and the third Test match stadium stamp, after Lansdowne and Twickenham, he would have on his rugby passport.

He wandered up to the gates and asked a security guard would he mind if he had a look around. The guard checked out Eoin's red tracksuit and frowned before asking him where he was from.

'Eh, Ireland,' Eoin responded. 'A place in Tipperary.'

'Ah, it's a long way to that place,' chuckled the guard. 'And that gets you a free pass, sonny. My old man used to sing that song. The guy that built Eden Park, his family was from there too.'

'Really?' asked Eoin.

'Yeah, a guy called Harry Ryan – Ryan's Folly they called this place once when it was just a cricket ground. But it's the biggest stadium in New Zealand now, so they're not laughing at Harry any more. Have a quick look around, but I'm knocking off in half an hour so be back here by then.'

Eoin thanked him and entered the ground, which was a bright, concrete modern stadium, unlike the one he had seen in the books his grandad had shown him before he left. He wandered around, soaking up the atmosphere and imagining the great deeds that had been done out on the field by All Black sides – and occasionally by their visitors.

He checked his watch and decided to head back to the gate, but on his way around the back of the grandstands he came across a statue that made his jaw drop. There, cast in bronze, was the great All Black, Dave Gallaher. Dave was one of Eoin's ghostly friends, a sporting legend who had joined him on an adventure a couple of years before. Amazed at the coincidence, he checked the inscription on the statue, which confirmed that it was indeed Dave Gallaher, and also told the story of how the rugby hero had volunteered to fight in a war from which he never came home.

Eoin grinned and rubbed the statue's toe for luck, before turning on his heels and heading back to the hotel.

CHAPTER 7

The first game of the tour was against Auckland Schools, and the local newspapers and TV were promoting the game as 'the unofficial Third Test' of the tour. The night before the game, Geoff warned them that Auckland would be the strongest of the schools' sides they would meet, and explained that as it was a short tour he was going to play his strongest side in the three Saturday games, and everyone else would start in the midweek fixtures.

Eoin reckoned that made sense, but he was less keen on the idea when the coach read out the fifteen to play the first game. Starting at No. 10 was an English player, Joe McGuinness from Manchester.

Eoin turned red, and then looked at the

floor. He knew almost everyone in the room was looking at him. Even Joe.

That he was on the replacement bench was only a small consolation to Eoin, but he raised his head and nodded as his name was called out.

'That's bonkers,' Paddy told Eoin as the players trooped out of the team room. 'You were player of the tournament in the Four Nations; you were the star of the World Cup; what more can you do?'

Eoin shrugged and bit his lip.

'Well, Geoff obviously has his own ideas. I'm on the bench, and we have the midweek games too. I have a chance to show him what he's missing.'

Joe tapped Eoin on the shoulder.

'That was as big a shock to me as it was to you,' he said.

'Ah Joe, don't worry about it, and go out there and take your chance. It's a team game and I want this side to win every match on this tour – and that means you playing well.'

Joe grinned and thanked him, but Eoin still stung from the injustice of the selection.

'What's that all about?' he asked Charlie as they had a bite in the restaurant later.

'I don't know,' replied the captain. 'I can't really discuss what I heard in the selection meeting, but you need to know that the other coaches were just as shocked at first when Geoff told us the side he wanted. Neil fought your case hard, but Geoff is the head coach, and the others gave in eventually.'

Eoin didn't sleep very well – he was still feeling the effects of the long flight and his pride had been hurt by being left out of the first game. He checked the time – 6.05am – and decided he would go for a run. As he passed the team room he had an idea, and ducked inside to borrow a couple of balls.

He felt a bit foolish jogging in the moonlight through the streets of Auckland with a rugby ball under each arm, and his red training top attracted plenty of beeping car horns and even some cat-calls.

He ignored them all, and made his way again to Eden Park stadium. The gates were locked, but Eoin found a quiet corner and shimmied up and over the wall.

Feeling a rush of excitement, he made straight for the playing area. Dawn was starting to show on the horizon, casting a slightly orange tinge on the glass stadium. It reminded him a bit of the Aviva in Dublin, a ground he had very happy memories of. He hoped he would get the chance to create a few more here.

He teed up the balls on the ten-metre line and did a few stretches to warm up his muscles. He jogged down to the other goal posts and back, before he took aim with his first practice kick. The ball split the posts, but as he was sizing up the second kick, the first ball came firing back at him.

'What the …' uttered Eoin. 'It must have hit something hard and come straight back. Weird.'

He took the second kick, and this time the ball went in off the upright and dropped into the in-goal area. Eoin was much more surprised when this, too, came straight back as if it had been kicked at him.

Dawn had broken, but Eoin still couldn't see what was causing the balls to boomerang back to him. He teed up the first one again, smashed it over the bar, watched as it ricocheted around the grandstand, and then waited.

Sure enough, a few seconds later the ball came hurtling back at him.

'Who's there?' called Eoin.

He heard a chuckling coming nearer, but still couldn't see anything until he asked again who was there.

Then right in front of him, a man in a black shirt and long black shorts appeared. He twirled his moustache and bowed to Eoin.

'Mr Madden,' smiled the figure. 'Welcome to Auckland.'

Chapter 8

'Dave!' laughed Eoin as he recognised the ghostly All Black legend. 'That was you messing around with the balls?'

Dave grinned back at him. 'I was just having a bit of sport with you. What has you in Auckland?'

'I'm here with a sort of mini Lions tour. We're called the Cubs.'

'Nice. I played in Wellington against the British Isles team, as they were called, back in 1904. They'd won all their games in Australia but we sent them home with their tails between their legs.'

'Well … we've only been together for four days so I don't expect we'll do too well, but New Zealand seems like a great place to play rugby.'

'It is, as long as you don't expect to win.'

Eoin laughed. 'So, what has you knocking around Eden Park?' he asked.

'This was my old stomping ground when I played. We were unbeaten for six years at one stage so I love coming back here. But I haven't been for a long time – those glass walls are new – so it must have been your presence that brought me here.'

Eoin wondered yet again about his knack of summoning spirits, usually long-dead ghosts of rugby players.

'Well, I rubbed the toe on your statue … I hope there's no major drama on this tour, it's bad enough being dropped.'

'Dropped? I thought you were quite the star these days. Brian Hanrahan keeps me informed of your progress when we meet up. I'm sure you'll fight your way back – I know you have it in you.'

Dave said he'd catch up again with him

later, so Eoin returned to his place-kicking practice. He kept it up for more than an hour, much to the shock of the security guard who opened the stadium at eight o'clock.

'Oi, what are you doing out there?' called the guard. When he recognised Eoin and his voice he became more friendly. 'Have you been here all night?'

Eoin laughed, and apologised.

'Sorry sir, I was out for a jog and decided to test your fences. Not too hard to scale, I'm afraid,' he grinned as he slipped out the main gate.

'Cheeky pup,' laughed the guard. 'I hope the schools give you a stuffing later.'

The security guard got his wish as a disjointed Cubs side, some of whom looked exhausted before the game started, were thrashed 33-12 by Auckland Schools. Eoin came on to replace Joe for the last fifteen minutes, and he scored and set up the only two tries the Cubs managed in the whole game.

But afterwards, Geoff was unrepentant.

'Well played everyone,' he began. 'That was a very strong Auckland side, and it's clear that a lot of you are still jet-lagged. We haven't had a chance to get used to each other and the calls and moves we're using, but I thought you did very well. A special word of praise to Joe who, despite the chaos all around him, managed to run the game brilliantly and lay the foundations for the two late tries. We're on our way back.'

Eoin kept his face as straight as possible, but a few others winced at the remarks.

'He's got to be joking,' said Paddy, back at the hotel. 'Joe's a decent player but there wasn't even one minute when he was running the game brilliantly out there. And then for Geoff to praise him for YOUR tries!'

Eoin shrugged and came out with the usual line about hoping to get a chance to show what he could do, but he was feeling pretty disheartened by the game – and Geoff's comments.

'I might as well come home now,' he told his best friend, Alan, in an email he sent before he went to bed. 'No matter what I do I'm not going to get on the team.'

Chapter 9

Next morning the team flew almost the length of New Zealand, a two-hour flight to the city of Dunedin.

'This is a bit like going home,' Alistair Dods told Eoin as they walked down the steps from the plane. 'I'm from Edinburgh, and the Scots Gaelic for that is Dùn Èideann. There's loads of Scots living here.'

'Well you won't get me in a kilt, no matter what,' laughed Rory as he joined them on the tarmac, where a group of native New Zealanders prepared to give them a typical Māori welcome.

'I don't think I like this Haka thing,' grumbled Charlie. 'It's grand doing it here, as a sort of cultural thing, but doing it out on the field is just done to intimidate the opposition.'

The boys watched as the Māori warriors lined up to begin the dance. Paddy walked right up in front of them and placed BIL on the ground before retreating.

The Haka, a traditional wardance of the native people of New Zealand, was a way to boast of the dancers' strength and intimidate the opposition. The mixture of chanting, thigh-slapping and face-making was finished off by a leap in the air. Eoin liked the pageantry of it, and loved the tradition it honoured, but he shared Charlie's misgivings.

Later, in his hotel room, he repeated his views in an email to Alan. 'I've been looking at YouTube, and some teams turn their backs on them, or get really close, but none of that solves the problem of it being an unfair advantage. Have you picked up any ideas on that course, Mr Analyst Man?'

Alan had been a great help to Eoin and his

teams, working out stats and other pointers that showed the strengths and weaknesses of their team and the opposition, perhaps he would know of a way that might help.

Eoin knew he would be starting the next game and resolved to make sure he was in peak form so as not to give Geoff any excuse. The following morning, they trained very early so they could take a bus journey across the country to the famous Queens-town. Rory was particularly excited as he was a big fan of the *Lord of the Rings* movies that had been filmed near there. Eoin wasn't as impressed with the scenery, reckoning he came from one of the most beautiful places on earth anyway, but he enjoyed the day off, dozing on the bus and chatting with Tayo and some of the Welsh guys.

Paddy wandered up and down the aisle of the bus, carrying his giant lion with him all the time. Eoin could tell the joke had worn off for him and he was fed up with his chore.

'Here, give me that beast for a while, you look like you need a break,' he told him.

'Can I trust you, Eoin?' Paddy grinned. 'Everyone else tries to snatch him, or hide him under the seats. I've a crick in my neck from looking for him.'

'He'll be fine,' laughed Eoin. 'I promise I won't let go of him.'

The day passed pleasantly, and Rory got to see the sights he wanted to see, before they pulled in to their hotel just as night fell.

CHAPTER 10

The South Island Schools XV proved to be poor opposition for the Cubs, who ran out easy winners. Eoin was happy with his own game, kicking six conversions and getting his talented back line running. He capped it off with a classy break, which let him in for a solo try just as the referee blew for full-time.

But if he was hoping for lavish praise from the coach, he was mistaken.

'OK, well they weren't much of a side, really,' sniffed Geoff in the changing room afterwards. 'I'm not sure that has given the coaches much food for thought. However, it is good to see the second-rank players fit and in form to keep the first choices on their toes.'

'Second-rank?' gasped Paddy, loud enough to be heard by almost everyone. He was only saying what most of the squad were thinking.

'We're travelling up to Christchurch in the morning, so make sure you get your sleep,' added Geoff.

Eoin didn't sleep well at all, his simmering anger ensuring he couldn't calm down enough to rest.

'You know I'm not one to complain,' he told Charlie in their room that night, 'but this just isn't fair.'

'I know, I know,' sighed his captain, 'and I assure you there has been much discussion of this in the selection meetings. But Geoff is just a huge fan of Joe and he won't hear anything said against him. We had very little chance of winning this series coming out here but now it's almost zero.'

'I wouldn't say that,' said Eoin, 'and I

really wouldn't say it if I was the captain!'

Charlie grinned. 'I know, I know, but it's hard to stay upbeat, especially when the coach has as much brains as one of those Orcs we saw in Queenstown.'

Eoin laughed. 'Look, we'll give it our best shot. I enjoyed getting out there today and testing ourselves. And what a kick it is to wear the red jersey. If I stick with rugby I think I'll revise my ultimate ambition from playing for Ireland to touring here with the Lions.'

Charlie nodded. 'Well, no matter what Geoff thinks, you're probably the one in this whole squad who'd be most likely to do so.'

As soon as they got settled in Christchurch, Eoin decided to follow his new habit and set off on a run in search of the rugby stadium. On the plane, he had learnt that a new stadium had to be built after a devastating earthquake in the city, but his route took him to the old ground, Lancaster Park. He had read a lot about old Lions tours and this was the venue for many famous games.

Eoin was shocked to see the state of the old stadium. A rusty padlock blocked the entrance, but it was easy to find a gap in the temporary fencing. Grass and weeds overran the place, and he peeked down the tunnel towards the pitch, where it was clear the grass hadn't been tended in years. There were huge cracks in the walls so Eoin backed away and made to leave.

'This was another of my haunts, if you excuse the term,' came a voice. Eoin turned around to see, once again, Dave Gallaher.

'I played here many a time against our great rivals Canterbury. Sad to see it falling down like this.'

'Are they going to fix it?' asked Eoin.

'No, sadly not. It's just too damaged to fix, I believe. They've already built a new ground and this one's for the demolition ball someday soon. It's full of memories for me,' added the All Black, before lowering his head.

'Well if it's too dangerous, they can't leave it like this,' suggested Eoin. 'But maybe they'll build something like a park you could come visit. And there's still plenty of grounds you played in that are still standing.'

Dave grinned back at him. 'There are indeed. And I hope we'll be seeing you in Eden Park next week.'

Eoin sighed and told him his problem with Geoff hadn't been solved.

'Well, that's tricky, but when I was a coach I was always impressed when I dropped a chap if he didn't sulk but instead went off and trained harder.'

Eoin nodded, and explained that was exactly his plan.

'The trouble is, though, this is such a short tour there's probably not enough time to change Geoff's mind.'

CHAPTER 11

The AMI Stadium was venue for the First Test and Eoin got to know it well over the next couple of days. He practised goal kicks every day, only stopping for a break when he had put over twenty successful kicks in a row.

The newspapers and TV devoted lots of coverage to the match, but Eoin found an excuse to keep away from the media day, when reporters came to the hotel to interview the players. He didn't fancy the attention that might come his way over the World Cup saga back home, but he also didn't fancy trying to explain why he wasn't in the starting fifteen.

In the dressing room before the game, Eoin hung back and let that lucky group take first pick of the benches, before he found one in the corner with Paddy and Rory. It was a weird feeling watching the team prepare for action, and even weirder seeing someone else pull the No 10 shirt over his head.

Rory ruffled his hair. 'I saw that look,' he said. 'Don't be worrying about Joe. Stay focused, be ready for action. We could be called in at any stage.'

Eoin smiled, and tied up his bootlaces just in time for Geoff and Charlie's final speeches.

Outside, Eoin joined the team for the warm-up, but moved to the sideline for the pre-match ceremonies. The stadium was almost full, with maybe 15,000 supporters all cheering for the Baby Blacks.

With two minutes to kick-off, the ref whistled for silence, and the tourists lined up, arm-in-arm, as the Kiwis prepared for their Haka. The boys recited the Māori chants, made the war-like gestures and leapt aggressively in the air, just yards from the Cubs.

Eoin watched closely as Charlie stood tall, eyeballing the New Zealand captain, Michael Wade, as he went through his moves. But Charlie didn't have much support, with several members of the team visibly taking a backward step and showing their fear.

Eoin muttered to Paddy. 'This isn't fair. They're getting a chance to intimidate us and we can't fight back.'

Just how much the side was intimidated became clear almost from the start, when a confident New Zealand were able to work the ball close to the Cubs line even before the first minute was up.

The Lions won the ball back and Joe cleared to touch, but the early evidence was starting to look grim for the visitors. The scoreboard rumbled into life and soon showed a 10-0 lead for the home side.

Eoin sat alongside Paddy on the bench, but he found it hard to watch. He was frustrated and annoyed at not getting out to play, but he also felt sorry for Charlie that his dream of leading a winning tour was going so badly wrong.

Ten minutes more and he was even starting to feel sorry for Joe. The out-half was too slow to escape the breakaway forwards and was getting hammered every time. Even when he got a kick away, it was rushed and failed to reach touch.

Thanks to some handling mistakes, the All Blacks were unable to take full advantage, but Michael Wade kicked a tricky penalty just before half-time to give them a 13-0 lead.

As Eoin stood up to follow the teams into the dressing rooms, he noticed Joe walking off chatting with Alistair Dods. But as he neared the tunnel, the out-half began to limp.

CHAPTER 12

'That's not too bad a position after such a slow start,' announced Geoff. 'We need to compete more in the breakdown, but with Joe playing so well we will have the platform to get back in the game.'

Eoin smiled, refusing to allow himself to react to Geoff's nonsense.

'Sorry Geoff' came Joe's voice from the other side of the room. 'I'm not sure I can carry on. I think I've done a hamstring.'

Everyone turned and looked at Joe, who was sitting on the bench with his leg stretched out. He was wincing with pain and rubbing his thigh. The physio rushed across and, with help from Neil, lifted him onto the treatment table before starting to work on the injured leg.

Geoff slapped his forehead and shrugged his shoulders, but Neil and the other coaches joined him in a huddle that sorted things out very quickly.

'Right. I have a plan,' said Geoff. 'We all hope Joe will be fit to take his place in the next seven or eight minutes, but should it come to the worst then we have Eoin Madden here to come in at 10.'

Matthew Peak couldn't help grinning, and Charlie flashed Eoin a thumbs-up, but Eoin kept his cool and didn't react at all, except to go into his pre-match routine. Geoff went off to talk to the forwards, and Eoin got his muscles moving with a few stretches. When the bell rang to signal a return to the pitch, Eoin saluted Joe McGuinness as he walked past the treatment table. Joe looked around to check that Geoff wasn't about, and returned Eoin's gesture with a grin – and a huge wink.

Eoin smiled as he trotted down the tunnel. Joe had made a sacrifice for the team, which was an incredibly generous action. Eoin knew he had better show he was worthy of it.

His arrival certainly gave a lift to his team-mates, and the Cubs tore into their opponents from the start of the second half. Oisín Deegan flattened the Kiwis' scrum-half, and the ball bounced free. After a scramble for possession, big Seán Nolan wrestled the ball back and presented it at the back of the ruck. Alistair Dods picked it up and made to go right before dipping low and squeezing past the cover on his left. He raced into space with only the full-back to beat. The No. 15 went low and hard, but as Alistair fell he fed the ball back to Dan Boyd, who collected it and ran in under the posts.

The crowd was stunned into silence, except for wild cheering from the tour party. Eoin slotted over the kick and another pen-alty goal five minutes later, to bring the Cubs deficit down to 13-10.

The Kiwis were rattled, and the coach panicked himself into bringing on six substitutes, including the whole front five as well as the full-back. But instead of improving the New Zealanders' performance, it spread confusion and even chaos.

Eoin spotted that the full-back, who usually played in the centre, kept advancing further up the field than he should have been. So the next time he had the ball in his hand he kicked it high into the air and over the full-back's head.

Eoin then charged off in pursuit, and with the full-back having to turn to follow him, he had a two-metre start. It was more than enough for Eoin, and he watched the bounce of the ball carefully before he collected it just inside the twenty-two but didn't slacken his pace until the ball was safely grounded under the crossbar.

Eoin took the congratulations of his team

and looked over to where his friends were sitting and chuckled as he saw Joe dancing on the seat. There didn't seem to be much wrong with his hamstring now.

Eoin and Michael Wade exchanged penalty goals, but, with four minutes left, the All Blacks were seven points adrift and besieging the British and Irish Cubs line.

Geoff used his last two substitutions. Eoin was dismayed that one of those going off was Seán Nolan, who had been having a massive game. His replacement, Harry Rees, was fresh and strong, but he didn't have the fight in him that made Seán such a key member of the team.

Sure enough, the next attack saw Wai Paenga, the giant Kiwi front row, break for a gap, but Harry didn't hit him hard enough and the black-shirt recovered to squirm forward and touch the ball down. The Cubs' heads fell. Their amazing comeback had been foiled and, as soon as the conversion went over, the sides were level. Both sides were so stunned and exhausted by their efforts that they went through the motions for the last forty seconds before the referee blew for full-time.

CHAPTER 13

'CLASSIC IN CHRISTCHURCH' read one newspaper headline next morning. 'CUB SUB SPARKS COMEBACK, BUT BABY BLACKS SALVAGE DRAW' went another.

Eoin yawned as he packed his bags. He was beginning to hate the cycle of packing, travelling, unpacking and hotel rooms that was the life of the touring sportsman or sportswoman. It had been an eye-opener for him and had caused him to think again about his career plans.

'I'm not sure I could stick this for a six- or eight-week tour,' he sighed to Matthew Peak, who had been his room-mate in Christchurch. 'By the time you've settled into a room it's time to move on.'

'Maybe you'll only have one more move so – I hear they're sending ten of the Test starters on to Auckland to prepare for the next Test. The rest of us are off to Wellington to play North Island Schools.'

'Really?' asked Eoin. 'No one's said anything to me …' He suddenly realised he wasn't a certain starter for the Second Test, no matter that he had almost single-handedly kept the series alive.

Down in the lobby, Geoff called them together to tell them the plan. He read out the list of names of those players who would skip the Wellington leg – and Eoin's name wasn't on it.

'We'll send Joe to Wellington so the physio can work on getting him fit for Auckland,' he announced. 'As he's been such a key player, we need to have him back to top fitness.'

Eoin felt a sinking feeling inside, knowing he would have to prove himself one last time to have any chance of starting the final Test.

Charlie came over to say goodbye, as he was among the group heading to Auckland with the coach. 'You're taking over as skipper for this leg, Eoin, if that's OK. Hopefully the game will go OK and you'll be in top form for Saturday. And don't worry, we'll be having a good row with Geoff if we need to.'

Neil took over as head coach for the North Island game, and the Cubs were a much happier bunch under his leadership. They enjoyed visiting the capital city, and training wasn't too hard, ahead of what would be the last game on tour for most of the side.

As the famous 'Cake Tin' stadium was too big for the expected crowd, the game was held at a club ground, which meant there was little protection from the gales. Wellington was windy almost all the time, which Eoin had found very tricky when practising his goal kicks the day before.

The Schools selection were big and brawny, but the All Black selectors were resting all their Test players to prepare for Saturday, so they didn't have much left by way of talent. The Cubs rattled in three tries in the first twenty minutes, but Eoin only managed one kick, and that was because it was in front of the posts.

At half-time the lead had already reached twenty-five points, so Neil replaced five of the boys who were also in the frame for the Test side. 'Geoff ordered me to give Joe a run-out to test his fitness so I'll bring you off in about ten minutes,' he told Eoin as the team prepared to run out for the second half.

Eoin put his heart and soul into the time he had left, realising it could be his last ever in the treasured red shirt. He passed, kicked and ran better than he had ever done before, and crowned his display with a solo run for a try. As he put over the kick Neil waved him ashore.

'That was magic,' he told Eoin as he pulled on a tracksuit. 'The game is being live-streamed on the internet so Geoff will be watching back in Auckland. I hope he agrees that you are the best man to start at 10.'

Eoin nodded, but decided not to reply in case he said the wrong thing. He was still fuming, but reckoned he had proved his case.

CHAPTER 14

The Cubs ran out 42-7 winners over the Schools selection. While Joe came through without any mishaps, the fast, exciting moves of the first half were missing, and the Cubs scored two tries towards the end only because the home side was tiring.

'I expect Geoff will say Joe was brilliant,' grumbled Tayo as they climbed on to the bus to the airport.

'Maybe,' sighed Eoin. 'But don't blame Joe. He's a nice lad and he doesn't want to be in that position either. He knows everyone thinks he doesn't deserve his place and that must be hard. He's been really nice to me too.'

Eoin sat next to Joe on the short flight to Auckland.

'I saw your wink in the dressing room,' he began. 'That was unbelievable.'

'Listen, Eoin,' Joe started, checking who was sitting close to them and lowering his voice. 'That was a no-brainer. It's embarrassing to me that Geoff sees me as the greatest thing since sliced … ham. I know my weaknesses and I know that you're a far better player than me.

'When we were in Dublin for the Four Nations you were head and shoulders above everyone else. I just hoped to get on the tour as a midweek player.'

'But you didn't need to fake the injury.'

'No, but if I hadn't we wouldn't have drawn that game. I wish Geoff would see that. I think he suspected that I wasn't really injured, but I'm a good actor!'

They chatted about their lives back home and what they had planned for the summer.

'Here we are,' noted Joe, as he looked out the window at Auckland below. 'This is set up for a fantastic decider. I hope you're ready for it.'

Eoin looked at him, puzzled. 'But, Geoff's not going to drop you …'

'He might have to,' grinned Joe.

The midweek team were ferried to the same hotel in Auckland where they had started their adventure a fortnight before. The rest of the squad were out training, so Eoin had some time to unpack for the last time and make himself at home in the room he had been drawn to share with Paddy this time round.

He stretched out on the bed and shut his eyes, but was soon awoken by his team-mate arriving back and dumping his kit bag loudly on the floor.

'I'm so browned off,' complained Paddy as he slumped down on his bed. 'That stupid lion has gone missing again.'

Eoin sat up and laughed. 'That's some welcome, Paddy, thanks!'

'Ah mate, I'm fed up. The lads have been kidnapping BIL every chance they get, but I always get him back. This time he's gone for two whole days and no sign of him anywhere. I get fined twenty dollars every day he's gone – and if he misses the Test I'll be broke. It's supposed to be awarded to the best player on Tour when we're going home so I'd hate someone to miss out on that souvenir.

'And it's really annoying – I was so careful with him. He disappeared from a locked dressing room at Eden Park while we were training. There was only ten of us and Geoff had the only key. I went mad looking for him, but all the guys swore they didn't take him.'

Eoin shrugged his shoulders. 'That's a real pain, Paddy. I'll go down with you to the stadium later and we'll have a look around.'

The boys caught up on the rest of the news from each half of the tour party, and Eoin checked his emails from home.

Mam and Dad had each sent him long emails full of news and concern that he was looking after himself and the usual worries that parents have when their child is on the other side of the world. Dixie sent him a two-line message wishing him luck and telling him to relax whenever he came on.

And Alan sent him an amazing email – his response to Eoin's complaint about the Haka. Eoin read it twice, and then showed it to Paddy. The pair grinned and headed for the door.

CHAPTER 15

As the boys trotted up to Eden Park, the stadium looked even more formidable than earlier in the tour, as if the looming Test match lent it a new air of menace. The sun was beginning to set, and the sky was a curious shade of pink and orange as they reached the main gate.

'Ah, the Tipperary man,' grinned the security guard. 'In for a look at where you want to be buried after Saturday's game?'

Eoin smiled back, and explained that he and Paddy wanted to have a look around as he had left something behind.

'No problem, your coach is around here somewhere too, just in case you need to avoid him.'

Eoin looked at Paddy and shrugged. 'We'll

keep a low profile. Maybe we'll duck into the museum here for a few minutes.'

The museum was small, but Eoin found plenty to keep him interested, especially about his old pal Dave Gallaher. He checked out the old All Blacks jerseys and the programmes from famous Tests against the Lions. There were trophies too – replicas of the World Cups from 1987, 2011 and 2015, and a plain wooden shield with a silver plaque in the middle.

'Hey, that's named after Dave,' said Paddy. 'The Gallaher Shield.'

The boys read about how it was awarded to the Auckland club champions and had been won most often by Dave's old club Ponsonby.

They left the museum and toured the stadium, giving the dressing rooms a good search – but with no luck. Paddy was getting more and more upset at his missing lion but there was no point searching any longer.

'Right, I'll take my punishment,' he sighed, and pointed towards the exit gate.

They exchanged more banter with the security guard before they decided to head back to the hotel.

Just as they left, Eoin had one last look back around the stadium concourse and was surprised to see Geoff slipping into the museum.

Next day saw the captains' run, a loose workout for the players at the stadium but no serious training. Geoff was a bit distracted and didn't talk to the team afterwards. Instead, he rushed off, saying he had to meet some New Zealand officials.

Neil told them the selection would be made that night and would be announced after dinner. He encouraged the boys to get out of the hotel and see a bit of Auckland as they would be flying home a few hours after the Test.

Eoin, Rory, Kuba and Charlie went for a stroll into the city and picked up a few souvenirs and presents for their families. Eoin bought an All Blacks shirt for Alan, and explained the plan his friend had suggested for the Haka. Charlie's eyes brightened and he chuckled as he thought it through.

'We'll go for it, remind me to get the guys to practise it in my room tonight.'

Joe was back in the team as first-choice No. 10, while everyone was delighted that Paddy had come in at inside centre.

There was a last night party in Charlie's room, although no one was in the mood to eat or drink too much. When the coaches left, Eoin explained Alan's suggestion and the players all agreed. After a couple of practices they all went off to their rooms in a good mood.

Eoin and Paddy sat up talking, but just before eleven o'clock there was a tap on the door.

'Dave,' said a surprised Eoin, as the ghostly All Black strode into the room. 'What has you here so late?'

Dave looked angry as he explained his visit to Eoin and Paddy, who was also able to see ghosts as long as he was with his friend.

'Look, I hear you guys were down in the museum yesterday, and you checked out the Gallaher Shield.'

'How do you know that?' asked Paddy.

'Harry Ryan here told me,' he answered, as the ghost of the Eden Park founder appeared at his shoulder, dressed in ancient cricket whites and a striped cap.

'Yeah, we were there for a while,' said Eoin. 'So what?'

'Well it's gone missing. Nearly a hundred years old and it's just disappeared.'

Eoin was shocked, and explained why he had visited Eden Park.

'There's a few things going missing around here, so,' said Harry.

'Well, keep your eyes open, Eoin, we could do with your help on this,' said Dave.

Chapter 16

The huge publicity about the tour – and the headlines about the stolen Gallaher Shield – ensured that Eden Park was packed with 50,000 fans, almost all of whom wore black. In the dressing room, Geoff gave a rambling talk to the team and ordered the scrum-half not to kick or run with the ball but to feed Joe. That was the final straw for the out-half.

'Geoff, this is rubbish. I'm no more the best out-half here than the man-in-the-moon,' Joe said before slipping the shirt off over his head and tossing it to Eoin. 'Cop yourself on and build your team around this guy. We've no chance otherwise.'

Geoff exploded, and the room went completely silent. Inside, Eoin groaned, but he was delighted that Joe had taken a stand.

'McGuinness, your mutiny is noted, and I will ensure you serve a long ban for this. But now, please put that shirt back on and get out there.'

Joe hesitated, but Eoin nodded to him and tossed back the shirt.

Geoff continued his talk, but just before the team left the changing room, Paddy stepped forward.

'Guys, this is the last chance – we won't be going out to play with our mascot unless someone owns up. Please, we need BIL.'

Nobody moved, but Eoin was stunned to see Dave Gallaher had appeared behind Geoff.

'I always changed in locker No. 1,' he called out to Eoin, who was the only one who could see or hear him this time. 'Check there.'

Eoin waited till the team had left and tried to open the locker, but to no avail. He grabbed a thin metal bar from the physio table, wedged it in the door and pushed hard. The locker sprang open, and BIL fell out with a thud.

Eoin grabbed the lion by his tail and raced out to join his team. 'Found him!' he called to Paddy, as he lobbed him the toy.

With a huge grin, Paddy put BIL on the centre line and watched as the Kiwis lined up to do the Haka. The Cubs linked arms and stared as the war-dance was completed, but as the ref blew his whistle for them to line up to start the game, Charlie strode up to halfway, followed by Ed Wood, Alistair Dods and Owain Morgan.

The crowd began to jeer, but Charlie raised his arms in the air and his men stepped forward one by one.

'I am of England,' bellowed Ed.

'Tha mi à Alba,' roared Alistair.

'Rwyf i o Gymru,' shouted Owain.

'Is Éireannach mise,' yelled Charlie, before

the rest of the team joined in, stomping around in a mixture of Morris Dancing and Riverdance, and all together they finished in a chorus that went:

We came from across the seas,
In a giant flying bird,
To conquer the land of the Kiwi.
Now, please … we say please … we say PLEASE,
Let's get back to the rugby.'

The crowd didn't know whether to laugh or boo, but in the end there was a warm round of applause as the Cubs lined up to start the game.

'That was fantastic – comedy gold,' grinned Neil on the bench. 'Was that your idea?'

'No,' replied Eoin. 'It was Alan. He's an international legend now.'

The Baby Blacks seemed a bit rattled by the Cubs' version of the Haka, and the visitors had a couple of early breaks, leading to Dan Boyd scoring in the corner. While the try was a great boost to the Cubs, they were stunned by Joe's awful attempt at a conversion, which trickled along the ground under the bar.

Joe turned and ran back towards the benches and, in frustration, aimed a kick at BIL.

'Owww!' he shrieked. 'That hurt'. And this time he wasn't acting.

The lion sailed through the air, and Eoin reached out to catch it. He was surprised how hard it felt.

'There's something inside,' he gasped, and Neil rushed over to investigate.

Neil primped and prodded the toy, and checked the stitching before carefully ripping it apart. He reached his hand inside and pulled out the Gallaher Shield.

CHAPTER 17

Eoin looked around and was astonished to see Geoff turn on his heels and run back down the tunnel. He pointed this out to Neil.

'Paddy and I saw him in the museum two days ago. He must have stolen it!'

Neil quickly conferred with the coaches, one of whom set off in pursuit of Geoff. The assistant coach took charge as play began again.

Eoin found a NZ Rugby official and returned the Shield, before resuming his seat on the bench. Michael Wade put over a penalty, but the Cubs were gifted a second try when Paddy nipped in to snatch a wild pass out of the air and run sixty metres to score. But even from in front of the posts

Joe couldn't add the points. He had winced in pain as he kicked, and ran straight to the touchline.

'Where's Geoff? I need to go off,' he gasped. 'I think I broke my toe off that stupid lion.'

Neil told Joe the coach had left, and signalled to Eoin to warm up. He trotted on with the score at 10–3 and ten minutes left in the first half.

Eoin was quickly into the action, slotting over a penalty, but the period running up to the break was all defensive doggedness. The Cubs' pack sat exhausted in the dressing room as Neil quickly explained why he was in charge and what the plan was for the second half.

Eoin slipped into the bathroom and bumped into Dave, who had a huge grin on his face. 'Thanks, Eoin. That meant a lot to me and Harry. Good luck today, even if it is the All Blacks you're playing. If I were you,

I'd test that new full-back Tipoki a lot more, he's windy under the high ball.'

Eoin thanked the ghost for his tip and raced out to join his team-mates on the field.

The Baby Blacks were fired up for the second half, and Eoin feared the ten-point margin wouldn't be enough. In Michael Wade he had a formidable opponent but he enjoyed the contest, especially when he sidestepped the Kiwi captain and left him flailing on the ground.

Eoin was always on the look-out for an opportunity to try out Dave's tip, and it came with fifteen minutes left to play and the score on 16-9. While the scrum was forming, Eoin ran forward to tell Charlie and Noah what he had in mind. When Owain flipped the ball back to him, Eoin swung his boot hard and high and the ball arched into the sky above Auckland.

The Cubs back row had peeled away quickly and were charging at full pelt towards the Baby Blacks' No. 15, Zinzan Tipoki. Trying to keep the ball in focus wasn't easy at the best of times, but with two rampaging Irish boys charging towards him, it proved too much for Zinzan.

He spilled the ball immediately, and slipped on the turf. It meant an easy run-in for Noah, but he paused at the line to pass to Charlie. 'Captain's honour,' he grinned, as he let Charlie touch down and the rest of the Cubs embraced them with delight. Eoin put the extra points on the board giving the tourists a 14-point margin which, despite an enormous effort by the Baby Blacks, remained the scoreline when the final whistle rang out.

Chapter 18

The Eden Park crowd were stunned at the defeat, and a few boos rang out, but slowly a round of applause built up before soon the whole stadium was saluting the victorious visitors. The Cubs waved back, and Paddy retrieved BIL from the sideline.

'Thanks, Eoin,' he laughed, 'for everything!'

Back in the dressing room, there were two policemen waiting, and Neil explained that they wanted to talk to Eoin and Paddy in particular, but also anyone else that had seen Geoff acting suspiciously.

Joe put up his hand. 'I think I know what he's been up to. Geoff knows my uncle, who's a dealer in rugby memorabilia. He was asking me about him on the way over here, and about how much he paid for famous trophies. I'm sure my uncle wouldn't buy stolen goods but Geoff might have thought he would.'

Everyone went silent as they considered how their coach had behaved.

'And I bet he had planned to award Player of the Tour to you, Joe,' said Paddy, 'and get you to smuggle the shield back home inside BIL.'

The policemen nodded, impressed that the youngsters had solved the case for them.

'He was picked up at the airport, you'll be glad to hear', said one. 'I'd say the Auckland prison rugby team will be delighted to get a new coach.'

After a suitable period of celebration at the ground, sharing some soft drinks and pizza with the Baby Blacks, it was time for the Cubs to say goodbye. Their suitcases were packed and loaded aboard the bus, so they went straight to the airport.

Half the side went straight to sleep on the plane, but Eoin and Charlie sat chatting as they waited for take-off. Neil called down to see everyone and got a huge cheer when he produced a holdall with BIL inside which he presented to Eoin.

Eoin grinned sheepishly and promised he'd look after it better than Paddy had, but his short speech was happily cut short by the announcement to take their seats and prepare for take-off.

Charlie peered over Eoin's shoulder and pointed out the floodlights of Eden Park as the plane wheeled over the city for the final time. Eoin smiled and the happy memories came flooding back.

'Thanks, Dave, and thanks, New Zealand, that was special. I'll be back.'

If you enjoyed *Rugby Roar* you'll love the rest of the series about Eoin Madden and his friends.

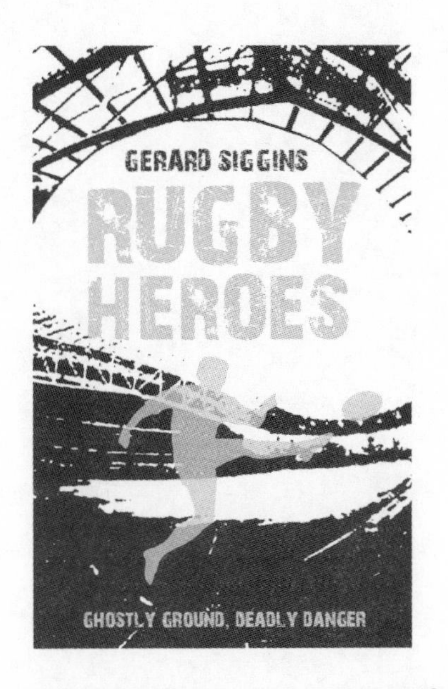

Turn the page to read an extract from *Rugby Heroes*.

Christmas was Eoin's favourite time of the year. He had a stack of memories of joyful mornings when he benefited from being the only child – and grandchild – in his family.

As he stretched out in his bed and lifted his legs over the side he wondered what delights would be under the tree for him this year.

Since he had started to do well at rugby there was no point asking Santa or his family for the usual presents of sportswear, as his wardrobe was stuffed solid with jerseys and tracksuits in both Leinster blue and Ireland green.

He had dropped a few hints about how he missed cycling since he'd outgrown his bike, and how good it might be to help him vary his fitness training. While he had been rested during the Mini World Cup he had borrowed a bike to get around the university campus and enjoyed the freedom it gave him.

Although it felt like so long ago, it was only a week or so since Ireland had won the final and Eoin had helped solve the mysterious theft of the William Webb Ellis Cup – with a little help from the man after whom the cup was named. Thinking of those days brought him back to the exciting moments of glory when Sam Farrelly had scored the winning try and Charlie Bermingham had lifted the trophy over his head. He felt a warm fuzzy glow rush through him and he jumped up from the bed, lifting an imaginary World Cup over his own head and taking the applause of the crowd.

He had been surrounded by newspaper reporters and cameramen after the game, but the Garda detectives had told him it was important he didn't say anything about the crime or the operation to recover the trophy as it might prevent the thieves from being sent to prison. Eoin was happy to keep quiet as he hated being the centre of attention anyway.

The IRFU was particularly delighted with his detective work, however, and he was chuffed when he got down home to Ormondstown for the holidays to find a letter of thanks from its president. He was even happier when he noticed that the paperclip on the top of the page was attached to four thin pieces of cardboard: 'Ireland versus England at Aviva Stadium, Saturday 30 March' was all Eoin bothered to read before he whooped with delight and rushed to show his mum.

He'd decided to say nothing to his grandfather, but instead slipped one ticket inside the pair of socks he always bought him for Christmas. That would be an excellent present!

Eoin dressed quickly and rushed down the stairs as quickly as he had every Christmas morning since he'd been able to walk. He popped his head into the kitchen, where his parents were already hard at work preparing breakfast and dinner.

'Happy Christmas, Mam, Happy Christmas, Dad!' he smiled. 'I wonder what's under the tree for me?'

He hugged his parents and handed over his gifts to them, before crossing to the sitting room, where a shining bicycle awaited him.

'Just what I wanted!'

'Why don't you run over to see Dixie?' suggested his mother. 'He's been on the phone already so he's up and about. Tell him your dad will collect him about one o'clock.'

'That would be great – but are you sure you don't want a hand peeling sprouts?' asked Eoin.

'Does the great detective Sherlock Holmes peel sprouts?' asked his dad. 'No, run on there and see your grandad.'

Eoin winced at what his father had said

– he really hated all the attention over the incident, and got particularly embarrassed when people called him a hero – but then he grinned gratefully and wheeled his bike out of the house, pausing to admire its perfect dark blue paintwork.

Eoin's grandfather, Dixie Madden, was once a great rugby player, and he had become Eoin's greatest supporter. He lived in a cottage nearby and Eoin called to see him every day he was home from boarding school.

'Hi, Grandad, Merry Christmas to you,' Eoin called as he spotted the old man opening the curtains at the window.

Dixie lifted his hand in salute and moved to open the door.

'Well, was Santa Claus good to you?' he asked.

'Very!' replied Eoin, hopping off and pointing to his brand-new bike.

'Oh, that's a beauty,' smiled Dixie. 'Does she move well?'

'Like a dream,' replied Eoin. 'I got over here in about two minutes flat.' He pointed to his watch. 'I've never run it faster than five.'

'That's good news. You'll have that bit more time to spend with me when you call over now,' Dixie chuckled.

'Dad says he'll call over at one o'clock,' Eoin said, as the old man ushered him inside.

'That will give us plenty of time to talk about rugby,' said Dixie. 'We will have to get that project of yours finished too.'

Eoin's face fell.

'Grandad … it's Christmas Day! You don't expect me to do school work today, do you?'

'Ah no, sure this isn't work at all,' laughed Dixie.

'Hmmm,' mused Eoin. 'It certainly sounds like it. What do you have in mind?'

'Well, your project is on the origins of

rugby and William Webb Ellis – the chap whose trophy you discovered. But besides Ellis spending some time here as a boy, there's nothing about the early days of rugby in Ireland. So, well, I thought you'd like this …' said Dixie, handing Eoin a parcel. 'I've a few other presents for you, but this will be useful.'

Eoin tore open the wrapping and saw that it was a book on the history of the rugby stadium on Lansdowne Road. He riffled through the pages, catching sight of old players whose names Dixie had mentioned to him. His friend Brian, too, had told him about the stars he had seen play at the ground.

'Wow, thanks Grandad. This is excellent,' he grinned. 'I promise I'll start reading it tonight.'

Dixie laughed. 'Well, I don't expect you'll allow it to get in the way of important Christmas things, such as eating and watching TV …'

After lunch, Eoin dished out presents – socks and chocs – but he especially enjoyed seeing the delight on his grandad's face when he saw there was a surprise bonus tucked inside. They made plans to meet up before the game and have a full day's fun with his parents.

The rest of the day flew by, but over the evening several visitors arrived, and each set wanted to hear Eoin recount his adventures at the final. He was delighted when the last of them left and, with a yawn, he said good night and hauled himself upstairs.

Eoin was tired and happy as he lay down on his bed. He reached over and picked up the book Dixie had given him and read through the early chapters before he decided it was time for sleep. He flicked on a few pages and was amazed to see there was a whole chapter on his friend Brian.

He had heard the story of the young Lansdowne player, and how he had lost his life, but it was still interesting to read about it in detail, and the book told him a lot more about Brian than the modest ghost had let on. Eoin read that Brian had been a seriously good prop, and had just been selected for the Leinster junior side to play Munster when he became the only player to lose his life playing on the ground. He grinned at how his friend had faced the same dilemma as he had in opting to play against his native province.

He studied the photo of Brian, amazed that he looked the same now as he had almost a century before. He felt a tinge of sadness that he wouldn't see his pal for a couple of weeks, and wondered what ghosts got up to over Christmas.

Eoin closed the book and nodded off quickly, sleeping deeply and soundly until a loud knock came to his front door early the next morning.

'Howya, Eoin!' came the call as he peered out the side of the curtain. 'Get down here and we'll go for a spin!'

Outside was his great friend and schoolmate Dylan, and he too was pointing at a shiny bicycle of the same make as Eoin's, although his was painted red.

'Santa got the rugby colours right, anyway,' chuckled Dylan as Eoin wheeled his own bike through the doorway.

Eoin was startled at what Dylan had noticed. Although he was from Munster, because he went to school in Leinster he had been selected to play for that province. It meant he got a bit of slagging thrown at him around Ormondstown, but he had got used to that and reckoned it was just some people's way of acknowledging his success. Still, he never wore a blue Leinster shirt around town, reckoning that might be just a little bit too provocative.

Dylan had no problem with wearing rugby shirts, though, and was rarely seen in school or over the holidays without the red

Munster shirt he had earned in the interprovincial championships the previous year. He was even wearing it today.

'I might repaint the bike green to keep them guessing,' laughed Eoin.

'But they'd think you were just being cocky about playing for Ireland,' frowned Dylan.

Eoin laughed. 'Yeah, you're right. Everyone has an opinion about me now that I've been on the TV news. I'll just paint it purple and hope nobody notices it's me cycling it.'

The pair rode around town twice, which didn't take very long. They stopped for a chat with Dylan's sister Caoimhe and her pals, who were out on their new bikes too.

'They'll have to put cycle lanes in Ormondstown soon,' laughed Dylan. 'Looks like everyone got a bike for Christmas.'

'I saw you in the paper for rescuing that trophy,' said Iris McCabe. 'You were very brave.'

Eoin blushed and laughed it off. 'I didn't

do much, I was in the back of a Garda car when all the action happened.'

'The papers said you were a "brave schoolboy star",' chuckled Caoimhe. 'I cut it out for you in case you missed it.'

'Did you stick it in the scrapbook you have about him?' asked Iris.

Eoin and Caoimhe blushed, and Eoin changed the subject.

'I wonder is there anywhere we could buy locks for the bikes?' asked Eoin. 'I wouldn't leave them out around town without being chained up.'

'I'd say you'd be all right,' said Iris. 'Sure, everyone knows everyone in this town. No one would steal from their neighbours, would they?

We hope you enjoyed this book.

Proudly brought to you by WORLD BOOK DAY,

the **BIGGEST CELEBRATION** of the **magic** and **fun** of **storytelling**.

We are the **bringer of books to readers** everywhere

and a **charity** on a **MISSION**

to take you on a READING JOURNEY.

EXPLORE new worlds (and bookshops!)

EXPAND your imagination

DISCOVER some of the very best authors and illustrators with us.

A **LOVE OF READING** is one of life's greatest gifts.

And this book is **OUR gift to YOU**.

HAPPY READING.
HAPPY WORLD BOOK DAY!

Illustrations © Jim Field